LITTLE SIMON
An imprint of Simon & Schuster Children's Publishing Division • 1230 Avenue of the Americas, New York, New York 10020 • First Little Simon paperback edition September 2022 • Copyright © 2022 by Simon & Schuster, Inc. All rights reserved, including the right of reproduction in whole or in part in any form. LITTLE SIMON is a registered trademark of Simon & Schuster, Inc., and associated colophon is a trademark of Simon & Schuster, Inc. For information about special discounts for bulk purchases, please contact Simon & Schuster Special Sales at 1-866-506-1949 or business@simonandschuster.com. The Simon & Schuster Speakers Bureau can bring authors to your live event. For more information or to book an event contact the Simon & Schuster Speakers Bureau at 1-866-248-3049 or visit our website at www.simonspeakers.com.
Series designed by Laura Roode.
Book designed by Chani Yammer. The text of this book was set in Usherwood.
Manufactured in the United States of America 0722 LAK 10 9 8 7 6 5 4 3 2 1
Cataloging-in-Publication Data is available for this title from the Library of Congress.
ISBN 978-1-6659-1923-4 (hc)
ISBN 978-1-6659-1922-7 (pbk)
ISBN 978-1-6659-1924-1 (ebook)

the adventures of
SOPHiE MOUSE

19

The whispering woods

By Poppy Green • Illustrated by Jennifer A. Bell

LITTLE SIMON

New York London Toronto Sydney New Delhi

Contents

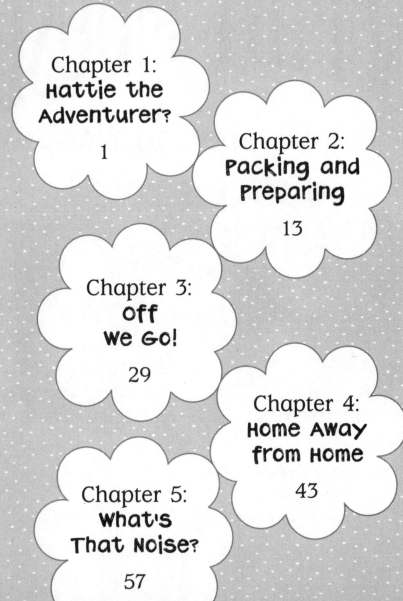

Chapter 1

Hattie the Adventurer?

Sophie Mouse was having a great Monday.

First, her mom had made maple nut pancakes for breakfast.

Next, at school Sophie's teacher had given the class an extra recess. "You all did so well on your math quiz! Go enjoy some time outside!" Mrs. Wise had said.

Then, Sophie remembered her acorn jacks were in her pocket. She showed them to her friends Hattie Frog and Owen Snake. "Want to play?" Sophie asked.

Hattie and Owen nodded eagerly.

So the three friends sat down next to the hopscotch court. Owen went first. He had to bounce the ball and grab the jacks with his tail—and he was surprisingly good. He got all the way to foursies!

Hattie went next. She got up to fivesies. Then she missed one jack.

Sophie went last. She almost messed up on twosies. But after that, she breezed right through tensies. Sophie won! It felt like her lucky day.

"Let's play again," said Hattie. She was eager for a rematch. "I'll go first this time."

While Hattie got ready, Sophie overheard her classmates in the hop-scotch line. Ellie Squirrel was talking about going camping.

"Really?" said Zoe, a bluebird. "Like sleeping outside?"

Malcolm Mole shook his head. "No way," he said. "I don't like the idea of sleeping on the ground."

Sophie giggled. Didn't Malcolm sleep *under* the ground?

Owen must have overheard the others too, because he nudged Sophie. "Have you ever been camping?" Owen asked.

Sophie shook her head. "Nope."

"I have!" Hattie exclaimed. "At this campground called Pine Crest. I've gone a few times with my family."

Owen's eyes lit up. "What's it like?" he asked Hattie.

Hattie thought for a second. "It's fun! And something *always* happens that makes for a good story." Hattie laughed. "Like last time, Lydie got our tarp stuck up in a tree. It was snagged on a branch. Lydie had to stand on my dad's shoulders to reach it. And when the tarp came loose, it fell on top of them!"

Hattie giggled. She described her dad and sister stumbling around like a very tall ghost.

The image made Sophie and Owen laugh too.

"Hey!" Hattie said suddenly. "What if we three went camping?"

Sophie frowned. "Just us?" she asked. "By ourselves?" She was a little surprised. Hattie was usually the cautious friend. Sometimes she got scared easily. And she wasn't always up for an adventure.

But Hattie looked so excited. And so did Owen.

"Lydie was allowed to camp out with friends when she was my age," Hattie said. "I know how to safely build a campfire. I know the best trail to the campground. I *think* I know how to put up a tent. But I can practice that."

"I don't know how to do any of those things," said Owen. "But I'm ready to help. Let's do it! How about next weekend?"

Sophie smiled. It was hard not to be excited when her *friends* were so excited. "Okay!" she agreed. "Let's go camping!"

— Chapter 2 —

Packing and Preparing

The friends had the week to prepare.

On Tuesday, Hattie made a list of everything they would need. She showed it to Sophie and Owen after school.

"We can use my family's tent," Hattie said. "Do you each have a sleeping bag?"

Sophie and Owen nodded.

"Backpacks?" Hattie asked.

Sophie had one. Owen didn't. Backpacks didn't really work for snakes. They decided Owen could pull a wagon. They could fit lots of stuff inside.

On Wednesday, they looked carefully at a map of Silverlake Forest.

They marked the trails they would take to get to Pine Crest. They'd have to go around Forget-Me-Not Lake, one of their favorite spots!

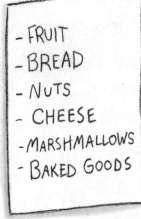

- FRUIT
- BREAD
- NUTS
- CHEESE
- MARSHMALLOWS
- BAKED GOODS

They made a food list on Thursday. "We *have* to bring marshmallows!" Hattie said firmly. "We'll want to roast them over the campfire."

"Oooh," said Sophie, "and I bet my mom might have some baked goodies we could take." Her mom, Lily Mouse, owned the bakery in Pine Needle Grove. And it wasn't just her maple nut pancakes that were amazing.

On Friday, Hattie and Owen came
over to Sophie's house so they could
practice setting up the tent.

Hattie took out the tent poles. "I think this goes through here," she said. She threaded one pole through a channel in the fabric. "Then this end goes here. And this end goes here." Hattie wrestled with the tent for a few minutes.

Sophie frowned. "Can we help?" she asked.

"No, I think I've got it," Hattie replied. "There!"

Hattie stood back to look at her
work. The tent poles stuck out at odd
angles.

"Cool," said Owen
supportively. "How
do we get in?"

Hattie's shoulders

fell. "Oh, it's all wrong,"
she moaned. "I don't
remember how
to do it."

Sophie tugged
at her whiskers. "Wait
here," she told them.
"I have an idea."

Sophie ran inside
her house. Her dad
was in the kitchen.

"Dad?" Sophie said. "Can you help us with . . . a building project?"

George Mouse came outside with her. "Ah, yes. Tents can be tricky," said Mr. Mouse. He lifted up one of the tent flaps to take a closer look. "Oh! I see the problem."

Sophie knew her dad could help.
He was an architect. He could design
big, sturdy structures. But he also
just loved putting things together.

Mr. Mouse adjusted one of the
poles. Hattie studied what he was
doing.

"There! You were very close!" he told them.

Hattie smiled. "I think I've got it now," she said.

Owen slithered around the tent. "Awesome!" he exclaimed. Then he ducked inside to look around.

But Hattie didn't notice him. Now that she knew how to set the tent up, she started taking it down. As she pulled out one of the tent poles, the fabric collapsed onto Owen.

"Aaaaaah!" Owen cried. "I can't see!" He wriggled around inside the tent.

"Oops!" Hattie exclaimed. "Sorry!"
She and Sophie lifted and pulled at
the tent, trying to find the opening.

Just then, Sophie's little brother,
Winston, came over to see what was
going on. His eyes fell on the myste-
rious wriggling shape.

Winston screamed and ducked behind Mr. Mouse. "What is it?" he cried.

Sophie, Hattie, and Mr. Mouse laughed. "Don't worry, Winston," Sophie said. "It's just—"

"Me!" Owen cried as he poked his head out of the tent. He slithered out. "Phew! I was starting to think I'd have to camp out in your backyard forever!"

— Chapter 3 —

off
we go!

On Saturday, the campers—and their parents—met up at Hattie's house. Mr. and Mrs. Frog made a big, hearty breakfast for everyone. There were berries and scones and maple yogurt.

When they were all done eating, Hattie checked and double-checked her lists. "We can't forget anything important!" she said.

Mrs. Frog patted her on the back.
"If you do, you can always come back
and get it," she said. "You won't be
that far away."

Hattie pouted. "But that would
ruin the adventure!" she said.

Sophie laughed. "Well, I definitely think we have enough food," she said.

The wagon was filled with containers of apple muffins, oat crackers with sunflower butter, vegetable pot pies, and more.

Mrs. Mouse reached into her purse. "Oh! I almost forgot. Here's a fresh batch of scones." She handed a tin to Sophie.

Sophie gave her a hug. "Thanks, Mom," she said.

Finally, it was time to set off. A
few more hugs and waves, and the
three campers were tromping away
down the path they'd marked on
their map.

They followed it along the stream.
Then the path took a sharp turn into
the woods. It wound back and forth,
around big rocks and under fallen
trees.

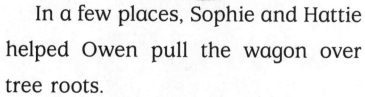

In a few places, Sophie and Hattie
helped Owen pull the wagon over
tree roots.

Eventually, they came to Forget-
Me-Not Lake. The blue flowers on
the grassy bank were in full bloom.

"Ah, I just love the lake," said Sophie. "Should we stop here for a bit?"

Hattie shook her head. "We have to get to the camp-site with plenty of time to set up before dark," she said.

"And plenty of time to have fun!" added Owen.

Sophie knew her friends were right. She followed them as they kept walking. But now she wondered about something. "Hattie, do you know what Lydie and her friends did for fun on their camping trip?"

Hattie nodded. "Lydie said they roasted marshmallows. So we've got that covered. And she said they told spooky stories about ghosts and noises in the woods."

Owen shivered. "Maybe we could skip that part," he suggested.

Sophie laughed. "Fine by me!" she replied.

"Oh!" Hattie said. She pulled something out of her pocket. It was silver and shiny.

"I almost forgot! I brought my harmonica. So we can sing campfire songs."

Sophie clapped her hands. "That sounds like fun!" she said.

As they walked on, Hattie listed the songs she could play on the harmonica.

"I don't know the words for most

of those," Sophie said. "Maybe you can teach us after dinner?"

"Yes!" said Hattie. Then she stopped in her tracks. As she stepped to one side, Sophie and Owen could see a wooden sign with big letters carved into it: PINE CREST CAMPGROUND.

Sophie cheered. "We're here!"

Home Away
from Home

"Look!" Sophie cried, pointing. There was a little box of cards attached to the signpost. The box had a label that said PLEASE TAKE ONE!

So Hattie took one. On one side there was a map of the campground. It showed the locations of campsites, picnic tables, firepits, nature trails, and the pond.

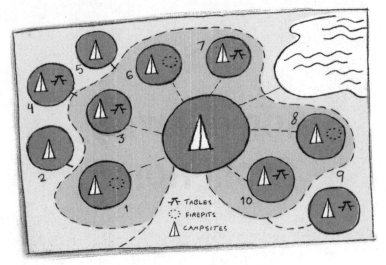

On the other side was a list of rules. Hattie cleared her throat and read out the first one: *"Treat the campground as if it is your home."*

"'No littering,'" said Owen, reading rule number two. *"'Pick up after yourself Whatever you bring in, please take out.'"*

Sophie went next. *"Please don't pick the flowers."* Too bad, thought Sophie. She often liked to collect flowers and plants. She used them to make new paints to use for her artwork. Oh well—she could find plenty of flowers to pick at home.

Hattie read the last rule. *"Take care of your fellow campers."*

"Aww," said Sophie. "That's nice." She looked around. "But . . . where *are* our fellow campers? It seems like we're the only ones here."

From where they were standing, they could see all of the main camp-site. It was green and peaceful—and empty. There were no other tents or backpacks or other camping stuff.

Owen nodded. "You're right. But it might be fun to have the whole place to ourselves!"

So the three friends set about finding a spot to set up their tent. The map showed ten different camp sites within the campground—they all were branching out from the main site. Sophie, Hattie, and Owen picked the second one they came to. It had its own picnic table and a stone firepit.

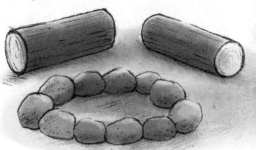

Sophie and Hattie put down their packs. Owen parked the wagon. They took out the tent and spread out all the poles. Hattie called out instructions, and to everyone's amazement, they got the tent up quickly!

Hattie stepped back to admire it. "Whew!" Hattie said. "I was nervous about that."

"It's perfect," said Sophie. "Our home away from home."

The friends put their food and other supplies inside the tent and zipped the front flap closed. Then they decided to have a look around.

They found the nature trail. They walked half of it, reading the signs about nearby trees and plants.

Then they came to a tree with a ladder attached to the trunk. Sophie looked up. Nestled in the branches was a wooden platform. It had three walls and a roof. "A tree house!" she exclaimed.

"Let's check it out!" Owen cried. He slithered up the ladder. Hattie and Sophie followed.

"Oh, I don't like heights," Hattie whimpered.

"But look at the view from up here!" Owen said.

They could see all
the way to the camp-
ground sign. They could
see the trail they'd walked
on. Beyond, they could even
see Forget-Me-Not Lake.
And they could see
that there was not another
camper anywhere in sight.

Chapter 5

What's That Noise?

"I have an idea. I'll be right back!" Sophie announced.

She climbed down the ladder and ran back to their tent. She grabbed one of the muffin tins. Then she brought it up into the tree house.

"Snack time!" she announced.

"Yes!" cried Owen.

The three friends were more tired

and hungry than they'd thought. They hadn't come that far from home, but the packs and wagon were heavy. The animals gobbled down the muffins and lazed in the tree house for a while.

Then Owen popped up with new energy. "What should we do next?" he asked.

Hattie checked the position of the sun in the sky. "Maybe it's time to set up for the evening," she said. "We need to find small sticks to get the campfire going. That's called kindling. Then we should hang up our tent lights so we can see after dark. And we should unroll our sleeping bags."

Sophie led the way down the ladder. At the base of the tree, she looked around. "Well, since we're already in the woods, let's get some kindling."

They wandered farther down the nature trail. Owen picked up a stick. "Is this a good size?" he asked Hattie.

"Yes," said Hattie. "And the drier the better. If it snaps in half easily, that's good."

Sophie saw a pile of fallen branches a little ways off the trail. She scurried in that direction. Owen followed Sophie. Hattie continued a little farther down the trail, but Sophie could still see her through the trees.

Sophie and
Owen picked up
about ten good
sticks. Then they
turned back toward the trail.

Just then, Hattie came running
through the trees. She was looking

behind her as she ran—and she nearly crashed into Owen! But she turned and saw him at the last second and skidded to a halt.

"Whoa!" Owen cried out. "Hattie, what's the matter?"

 Hattie's eyes were wide and her face was flushed. "Did you two hear that?" she asked, panting heavily.

Sophie and Owen looked at each other. Then they shrugged at Hattie.

"Hear what?" Sophie asked.

Hattie held up one hand. "Listen!" she whispered.

The three friends stood perfectly still in the middle of the woods. Sophie's ears twitched. They listened.

But the only sound was the breeze rustling the tree leaves.

"What did you hear?" Owen asked Hattie.

Hattie hesitated. "A . . . a rustling," she said.

"Oh!" Sophie said. "Well, I hear that. It's just the wind in the trees."

Hattie didn't look so sure. "No," she said. "It was a different rustling. Maybe. Or I don't know. I guess it could have been a sudden gust so it was louder." Hattie looked calmer now. She gave a weak smile.

Sophie smiled too. "*Maybe* you're just remembering a story Lydie told you? About hearing noises in the woods?"

Hattie took a deep breath and sighed. "Yes," she said, nodding. "That's probably it."

— Chapter 6 —

The Rustling Reeds

Sophie and Hattie carried the kindling back to the campsite. Along the way, Owen picked up a few more sticks with his tail.

They put some of it inside the firepit.

"Okay," Hattie said, "fire safety! Before we *start* a campfire, we need to have a way to put it out. Oh!" Hattie looked around. "Oh no."

"What?" asked Sophie.

Hattie pulled a bucket out of the wagon. "I forgot we need to get water. To fill the fire bucket. We need to keep it next to the campfire at all times."

Sophie took the bucket. "I'll get some!" she said. She didn't mind exploring a little bit more. And the stream was marked on the map. Sophie just had to go down the hill toward campsite number four. From there, she could follow the sound of the rushing water. So she set off.

Along the way, Sophie stopped a couple of times. She found a blueberry bush brimming with berries. She grabbed a couple and popped them into her mouth.

Then she spotted an interesting leaf on the ground. It was purplish and had curvy edges. Sophie put it in her pocket. If she couldn't pick flowers, maybe she could make a new paint color from the leaf.

At the stream, Sophie hopped onto a rock. She lowered the bucket down and the water rushed in. Sophie held on tight so the current didn't carry the bucket away.

Just then, she heard a noise on the far bank. Her ears perked up.

What was that?

She stood frozen to her spot. She held her breath, listening. All she could hear was the burbling stream. Sophie breathed out and reached down to pick up the bucket.

But then she heard it again. For sure this time. A rustling on the other side of the stream. *It's coming from those reeds,* Sophie thought.

So she left the bucket. Hopping
from stone to stone, Sophie crossed
the stream. But she couldn't see what
was on the other side of the reeds.
She waited again, silent and still.

Then, suddenly, Sophie bravely reached in. She pushed the reeds aside like a curtain and . . .

There was nothing there. Nothing but mud and stones and, farther up, the grassy bank.

Huh, thought Sophie. She would have bet that someone was there. But no one was.

So Sophie went back across the stream. She grabbed the bucket, now filled with water. Then she hurried back to the campsite. She walked a little faster than she had on the way there.

Was that the same sound Hattie heard? Sophie wondered. *Or thought she heard? And . . . did I really hear it?*

By the time she got back to camp, Sophie wasn't sure any-more. Reeds did rustle, after all.

Chapter 7

Mysterious Music

Sophie decided not to say anything to Hattie and Owen. She didn't know what she'd heard, and she didn't want to scare Hattie again.

Anyway, everything was cheerful once they got the campfire going. The friends set the picnic table and pulled out the veggie pot pies. They ate and laughed and talked about swimming in the pond the next morning.

After dinner, Hattie got out the marshmallows. Then she picked a good roasting stick from the pile of extra kindling. Sophie and Owen did the same.

Hattie showed them how she twirled her stick over the fire. "This way, the marshmallow gets evenly golden all around," Hattie said.

Sophie tried it, but dropped her first two into the fire. The third time was the charm.

Owen was too impatient to roast his marshmallow at all. He just ate it as is.

Hattie roasted one for him. "You have to have at least *one* roasted one!" she proclaimed.

"Mmm," said Owen as he chewed. "Thanks, Hattie."

Before long, they were full. They cleared the picnic table and put away the food.

Then Hattie pulled out her harmonica. "Ready for some campfire songs?" she asked.

Sophie and Owen cheered. They settled down in the campfire's glow as Hattie began to play. The lovely notes rose up into the darkening sky. Hattie was really good!

After the first few lines, Sophie recognized the song: "The Bear Went Over the Mountain."

Sophie and Owen started to sing along.

> *To see what he could see,*
> *To see what he could see.*
> *Oh, the bear went over*
> *the mountain,*
> *to see what he could see.*

As their last notes rang out, Sophie raised her hands to clap. But for just a second, she thought she still heard music.

Right then Owen clapped, and Sophie started to clap too. *Maybe it was just an echo*, thought Sophie. *Our song bouncing off the trees.*

Hattie and Owen didn't seem to hear it. Hattie was getting ready to play another tune.

"I think I remember 'Row, Row, Row Your Boat,'" she said.

She began to play. Again, Sophie
and Owen joined in. By the end, they
were singing quite loudly.

Merrily, merrily, merrily,
merrily, life is but a dream!
Their voices and the harmonica
stopped at the exact same time.

But there it was again: different musical notes wafting in from a distance. Sophie was sure!

Hattie and Owen turned to look in the direction of the music.

"Do you hear it too?" Sophie asked them.

They both nodded. "Music!" said Owen.

"But where is it coming from?" Hattie asked. "And who is making it?"

~ Chapter 8 ~

Follow That Sound!

Then, from the same direction, came a different sound: a loud, clattering crash!

"W-w-what was *that*?" said Owen. His voice was a little shaky, and his tail was quivering.

Sophie shook her head. "I don't know," she said. "But we should probably go check it out."

Sophie got up. But Hattie grabbed her arm.

"Sophie, wait!" Hattie cried. "We don't know what's out there."

Sophie paused, thinking. Hattie was right. But then she remembered one of the Pine Crest rules: Take care of your fellow campers.

"What if there *are* other campers here, after all?" Sophie said. "What if they need help?"

Hattie's grip on Sophie's arm loosened. She sighed. "Oh, all right," she said. She ran to the wagon and dug around in a sack. "But we're taking these!"

Hattie held up three flashlights. She gave one to Sophie and one to Owen.

The three friends stayed close to

one another. They agreed that the sounds had come from the woods. So they went that way. But for now, everything was quiet and still.

When they reached the nature trail, Sophie whispered, "This way?" She pointed down the trail.

"Okay," said Owen.

"I guess," Hattie added.

Slowly, they made their way forward. After a handful of steps, they'd stop and listen. And then they'd continue on.

Suddenly, from out of the darkness ahead, there was a thud and a sudden rustle. Like a branch falling into a pile of leaves . . . or something? The three friends jumped.

They aimed their flashlights this way and that. Sophie couldn't see what had caused the noise.

But her flashlight beam fell on a familiar shape: a ladder.

"The tree house," Sophie whispered. She hurried toward the base of the tree. "Come on! Maybe we can see better from above."

When the friends got to the top
of the ladder, they turned off their
flashlights. They sat silently, catch-
ing their breath. Sophie squinted into
the darkness, down toward the forest
floor. But she couldn't see anything.

"Okay," Sophie said. "Now turn
your flashlights back on."

There were several clicks as flash-lights went on all around Sophie. Wait. Too many clicks! Sophie blinked as the tree house got brighter and brighter.

Instead of just the three of them,
there were six!

"AAAAAAAAAAH!" Sophie, Owen,
and Hattie cried.

"AAAAAAAAAAH!" cried the others across the tree house platform.

~ Chapter 9 ~

Some Friendly Faces

Next to Sophie, Hattie and Owen were still yelling. But Sophie had stopped.

Her eyes were adjusting to the light. And now the faces looking back at her were familiar.

"Wait, wait, wait!" Sophie cried out.

The screaming stopped.

"It's Zoe," Sophie said. "And Malcolm and Ellie!" Their classmates from school!

"Sophie!" Ellie Squirrel cried out. "Oh, thank goodness. Owen! Hattie!"

Everyone breathed a sigh of relief. Hattie was still shaking a little. But even she started to laugh. And it was contagious. Soon, every one of them was giggling.

"What are you three doing here?" Malcolm asked.

"We're camping!" Sophie replied. She pointed in the direction of their campsite. "Our tent is right over there."

"But we heard music," Owen added. "Then a loud crash. So we came to investigate."

Malcolm and Ellie looked at Zoe.

"That was me," Zoe said sheepishly. "I was singing. Maybe too loudly. And dramatically. I flapped my wings and knocked our dishes out of the tree house."

Ellie explained that they were camping too. But way over at the other end of the campground. "We found this tree house earlier. We thought it would be fun to have our dinner up here."

Sophie looked around the tree house now and noticed that indeed there was a blanket and some food laid out. "But . . . why were you sitting here in the dark?" she asked.

Malcolm's eyes got wide. "We heard footsteps!" he cried. "Yours, I guess. So I turned off our lantern. But I dropped it. It fell down there into the leaves. Then we had to find our flashlights in the dark."

That explains the thud, Sophie thought. She thought back to Monday. That's when she had overheard Ellie, Zoe, and Malcolm talking about camping.

Sophie told them about that. Then she pointed to Malcolm and Zoe. "I thought I heard you two say you didn't like the idea."

Malcolm and Zoe shrugged. "We decided to give it a try," Zoe said.

The whole week, the two groups had been planning their own camping trips. To the same campground!

"I have an idea!" Hattie exclaimed. "Want us to help you move your tent over to our campsite?"

Ellie beamed. "That's a great idea! Especially because I'm not sure I set it up right. Maybe you can help us?"

Hattie nodded. "You bet!"

Chapter 10

The More
the Merrier

With four of the animals each
carrying a few things, and two light-
ing the way with flashlights, the
move was complete in no time.

Ellie's tent was similar to Hattie's,
so Hattie showed
her how to
position the
tent poles and . . .

"Ta-da!" Hattie said. It was ready
for move-in. Zoe, Malcolm, and Ellie
arranged their sleeping bags inside.

Then they all gathered around
the campfire.

Zoe pulled a recorder out of her pack. "Want to play a duet, Hattie?" she asked.

"Sure!" Hattie replied. She looked thrilled to have another musician in the group. "Do you know 'Twinkle, Twinkle, Little Star'?"

Zoe and Hattie began to play.
Then everyone joined in singing.

Sophie smiled and gazed up at the crystal clear night sky. She remembered what Hattie had said. That it would be fun to go camping. Hattie was right. And she'd said one other thing.

Something always happens that makes for a good story.

Yes, thought Sophie. *Hattie was right about that, too.*

The End

the adventures of
SOPHIE MOUSE

For excerpts, activities, and more about these adorable tales & tails, visit AdventuresofSophieMouse.com!

If you like Sophie Mouse, you'll love

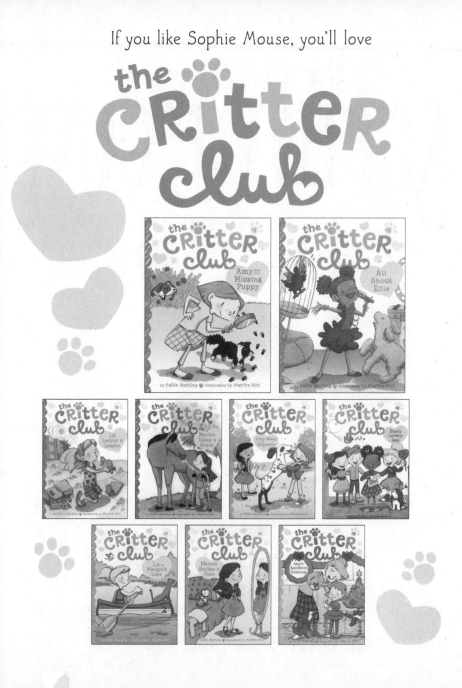